Thank you, Sev and Indy, for giving William the Monster outfit

Text and illustrations copyright © 2003 by John Wallace
All rights reserved. No part of this book may be reproduced or transmitted in any form or by any means,
electronic or mechanical, including photocopying, recording, or by any information storage and retrieval system, without
written permission from the publisher.
For information address Hyperion Books for Children, 114 Fifth Avenue, New York, New York 10011-5690.
First Edition
1 3 5 7 9 10 8 6 4 2
Printed in Singapore
Library of Congress Cataloging-in-Publication Data on file.
ISBN 0-7868-1996-0
Visit www.hyperionchildrensbooks.com

MONSTER
TODDLER

JOHN WALLACE

Hyperion Books for Children
New York

7

Charlotte had a lovely little brother,
Timothy, the sweetest boy in all the world.

But one day Timothy put on his monster suit . . .

and turned into . . .

MONSTER TODDLER!

The rascalliest boy
IN THE WORLD!

Monster Toddler
splashed his juice
all over Charlotte.

He leaped out at her.

He tried to bite the cat.

He broke Charlotte's
toy town.

He kicked the pieces
everywhere. . . .

Finally Charlotte hollered—
"You're driving me crazy!"

Charlotte ran to her room
and slammed the door.
"I'm not playing with you!"
she cried.

"Good!" said Monster Toddler.

"Because I can play . . .

BY
MYSELF!"

Oh, no!

Monster Toddler made such
a mess that he couldn't get out.

"Help me!" he called.
"I'm stuck!"

"**WONDER CHARLOTTE** TO THE RESCUE!" cried Charlotte as she burst out of her room. "I will help you, Monster Toddler, but only if you start to be good!"

"Good? What is good?" asked Monster Toddler.
"Let me show you," said Charlotte.

Charlotte showed
Monster Toddler
how to clean up, not
make a mess . . .

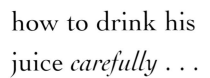

how to drink his
juice *carefully* . . .

how to sit
quietly and not
leap out . . .

how to fix
Charlotte's toy
town,

not break it . . .

and how to be
kind and gentle.

"Thank you for helping me!" said Monster Toddler.
"I like being good!"

"Well, now that you like being good, you don't need your monster suit, do you?" said Charlotte.

Charlotte helped Monster Toddler
take his monster suit off.

He looked quite
normal underneath.

In fact, he looked just
like Timothy . . .

Charlotte's lovely little brother,
the sweetest boy in all the world.